W9-ATD-636

DESPICABLE ME MINION MADE

Mower Minions

Adapted by Trey King • Illustrated by Ed Miller

(Based on *Mowers Minions* short, original Script by Glenn McCoy & Dave Rosenbaum)

LB kids

 • Little, Brown and Company • Hachette Book Group • 1290 Avenue of the Americas, New York, NY 10104 Visit us at lb-kids.com • LB kids is an imprint of Little, Brown and Company. The LB kids name and logo are trademarks of Hachette Book Group, Inc. • The publisher is not responsible for websites (or their content) that are not owned by the publisher. • First Edition: July 2016 • ISBN 978-0-316-39297-6 • 10 9 8 7 6 5 4 3 2 1 • CW • minionsmovie.com
Printed in the United States of America

What are the Minions doing on a lazy afternoon?
Watching TV, of course!

An amazing commercial comes on. It's an ad for Barb's Blender—great for making banana smoothies! The Minions *have* to have it!

How will the Minions get inside their piggy bank? They could use dynamite! (Or just a hammer.)

Inside, they find a quarter. That's not enough to buy the new blender!

Outside their window, they see Mrs. Rose paying
Larry for cleaning up her yard. That gives the Minions
a great idea!

The Minions borrow a lawn mower and some lawn tools from Larry. He won't mind, right? Now they just need to find their first customers.

Some residents sit on the front porch of a local retirement home. The Minions offer their new lawn services.

The residents are a little hard of hearing, but nonetheless, they hire the Minions to work on the yard. Time to get to work, Minions!

Dave takes charge and hops on the lawn mower.
How difficult can it be to drive one of those things?
It turns out...*very* hard. The mower is out of control!

VROOM

On the other side of the yard, Jerry rakes leaves when he bumps into a gnome.

Instantly, the two become locked in a staring contest!

The Minions are working hard...or are they hardly working?

Watch where you step, Dave. *Oops!* Too late.

Time for yard cleanup!

Uh-oh! Looks like the leafblower is blowing up someone's hazmat suit!

RRRRR

One Minion is running around with a beehive on his head.

Another turns green when he smells something yucky.

Another Minion is bouncing around the yard in a blown-up suit.

Another crashes the mower.

And another blows up the barbeque grill!

Bzzz

Bzzz

Bzzz

Bzzz

Bzzz

The Minions feel terrible. They were trying to do an honest day's work to earn money, but everything went wrong.

They go to the porch to apologize
to the residents of the home.

The people are laughing so hard, they can barely stand. "Thank you so much for that," says Gertrude. "That's the most we've laughed in a very long time."

"Here you go, young man," adds Gertrude. "Payment for a really funny show. Spend it wisely."

They did it! The Minions can buy their blender now! Hooray!

After a few days of using the blender nonstop to make banana smoothies, the Minions can barely move! They're *sooooo* full.

Wait! A new-and-*improved* blender? With an arm that peels the bananas for you? The Minions have to have it! Where are they going to get the money?

It's time for the Minions to get a *another* job!